Curious George
Ten Again and Again

Written by Francie Alexander

Houghton Mifflin Harcourt
Boston   New York

George is one curious monkey.
What is inside?

George will go to a party.

The man circles the date.

George and the man shop
for a present.

The man counts out the money.

The man counts out ten one-dollar bills and ten pennies.

It's party time!

Happy birthday!
Make a wish!
You are ten!

George is one tired monkey.
He counts ten sheep then
he's asleep.
Shhh!